THE BIG BOOK OF SMALL TO TALL POKÉMON

By Steve Foxe

A GOLDEN BOOK • NEW YORK

rhcbooks.com
ISBN 978-1-5247-7257-4
Printed in the United States of America
10 9 8 7 6 5 4 3 2

The regions of Kanto, Johto, Hoenn, Sinnoh, Unova, Kalos, and Alola are inhabited by special creatures known as Pokémon. Some are small enough to fit in the palm of your hand, and others are large enough to ride across the beaches, seas, and snowy mountain peaks of this world. Join Pokémon Trainer Ash and his companion, Pikachu, as they discover Pokémon ranging in size from the smallest Cutiefly to the most gargantuan Gyarados!

Many Pokémon tower over their Trainers, but others are small enough to fit in your pocket! These four Pokémon are among the tiniest discovered so far.

When Fairy-type **Flabébé** finds a flower it likes, it takes care of it and uses it as an energy source. Just as small but not quite as light is the tiny Bug- and Electric-type Pokémon **Joltik**. Joltik can't generate its own energy, so it attaches itself to larger Pokémon and draws out their static electricity.

Another challenger for the "Tiniest" crown is **Comfey**, a Fairy-type Pokémon that likes to gather delightful-smelling flowers to place on its vine. Like Comfey, **Cutiefly** is 4 inches tall—smaller than the flowers that attract this Pokémon! This Fairy- and Bug-type Pokémon can even detect which flowers are about to bloom. If a Cutiefly follows you, it might mean you have a floral aura!

WELCOME TO KANTO!

The Grass- and Poison-type **Bulbasaur** is the tallest of the Kanto first-partner Pokémon. While Bulbasaur naps in the sunshine, its seed soaks up the sun's rays and uses the energy to grow. Slightly shorter than Bulbasaur is the Fire-type **Charmander**, who is extremely popular among new Trainers. If Charmander's flame is burning brightly, watch out—it might be very angry!

If threatened in battle, Water-type Squirtle will tuck itself back into its tough shell, which is streamlined with a grooved surface to help Squirtle swim quickly. The smallest Pokémon of this bunch still packs a punch: I choose you, Pikachu! This Pokémon stores electricity in its cheek pouches and discharges it regularly to maintain good health. Ash's Pikachu proves that huge amounts of heart and courage can come in small packages.

To farmers, tiny Mole Pokémon **Diglett** can be both a blessing and a curse. Its burrowing helps prime the soil for growing crops . . . but it also occasionally chows down on plant roots! If the air feels chilly, that may be a sign that **Gengar** is about to attack. This Ghost- and Poison-type Pokémon tries to create kindred spirits by attacking humans! Since it's 4'11" and weighs 89.3 pounds, you might even mistake Gengar for one of your pals . . . until it's too late! **Arcanine** cuts an intimidating profile, standing over 6 feet tall with a flowing mane, and can run remarkable distances thanks to the flames that burn within it.

Even larger is **Lapras**, a majestic Water- and Ice-type giant of the waves. Because of Lapras's gentle personality and large size—it's over 8 feet tall and weighs nearly 500 pounds—many people ride on its back to cross the waters surrounding Alola and elsewhere, giving it the nickname of the Transport Pokémon.

WELCOME TO JOHTO!

As in Kanto, the first-partner Pokémon of this region come in small packages but can level up into truly mighty specimens. The tallest of the group, Grass-type Pokémon **Chikorita**, can wield its leaf fiercely during battle, driving away foes with a calming fragrance. If **Cyndaquil** is threatened, the flames on its back roar to life to scare off attackers. As it evolves, the flames on this fiery little Pokémon burn hotter and brighter.

Don't turn your back on Water-type **Totodile**—with its powerful jaws, it can take a bite out of anything. Totodile may think it's only playing, but those teeth are sharp! Totodile evolves into **Croconaw**, which evolves into **Feraligatr**, one of the largest evolutions of a first-partner Pokémon yet discovered. At more than 7 feet tall, Feraligatr scares most Pokémon even before revealing its intimidating teeth!

The teeny-tiny **Togepi** stores up happiness from other beings in its shell. This Fairy-type Pokémon gets its energy from positive emotions. Many other Johto Pokémon stand at human height or taller, like the Electric-type **Ampharos**, which is 4'07" and was used long ago to send signals over great distances due to the bright light it radiates from its tail.

Slowking is exactly 2 feet taller than Ampharos, but most of that difference can be attributed to its "crown." The Shellder on its head mysteriously unlocked Slowking's hidden wisdom. The mighty **Steelix** is more than 30 feet long and weighs 881.8 pounds! Don't worry about coming face to face with one of these giants, though: Steelix lives deep underground and can tunnel more than half a mile below the surface.

HEAVY HITTERS

Be careful around these heavy hitters! Even gentle giants can knock over a building or two if they're not careful.

Snorlax weighs more than 1,000 pounds, and eats nearly that much food per day! This Pokémon eats even when it is asleep. **Metagross** may be smaller than Snorlax, but its density helps it outweigh the sleepy behemoth. The Steel- and Psychic-type Pokémon uses its four massive arms to pin down foes.

The Alola region has its fair share of large-and-in-charge Pokémon. **Mudsdale** is the evolved form of Mudbray. This 2,028.3-pound Pokémon produces weather-resistant mud that coats its hooves. Its mighty kicks are strong enough to demolish a truck! Another Pokémon first spotted in Alola may be one of the smallest Pokémon in existence— and one of the heaviest! Despite fitting in the palm of your hand, **Cosmoem** weighs more than 2,000 pounds. Some people suspect that this miraculous unmoving Pokémon hails from another world.

WELCOME TO HOENN!

The first-partner Pokémon of this region are all on the smaller side, with none of them standing taller than 1'08"—but don't underestimate them!

Tiny Fire-type Pokémon **Torchic** is covered in soft feathers and has a fire burning in its belly, which makes it warm and snuggly to hug. But be careful—it can breathe flames and shoot fireballs when it's angry! Grass-type **Treecko** may be small, too, but it has a reputation for standing up to larger foes. Treecko has small hooks on its feet that allow it to climb walls.

Water-type **Mudkip**'s small stature hides its great strength. Its fin is extremely sensitive and helps it sense movement and potential danger. Mudkip evolves into **Marshtomp**, which evolves into **Swampert**.

If it trusts its Trainer and holds the correct Mega Stone while its Trainer has a Key Stone, it can Mega-Evolve into **Mega Swampert**. At 6'03", Mega Swampert is 2 feet taller than Swampert and much sturdier. Only the most powerful attacks will bother this river giant!

The land of Hoenn has native Pokémon of all sizes. **Aron** may be little, but it weighs as much as a human adult. It can destroy a heavy truck with a full-speed charge! **Kecleon**, the Color Swap Pokémon, is a master of camouflage and can change color to blend into almost any environment, but the zigzag pattern on its stomach always stays the same.

The hefty **Slaking** may be the world's laziest Pokémon. It spends most of its life lying on its side, and will only move if it runs out of food within its reach. At more than 7 feet tall, **Hariyama** towers over all but the tallest Trainers. This Fighting-type Pokémon's open-palm strikes can toss full-sized trucks into the air! Luckily, Hariyama prefer to focus their energy and strength on training Makuhita rather than fighting each other.

WELCOME TO SINNOH!

The Water-type Penguin Pokémon **Piplup** prides itself on its independence. It's only 1'04" tall, but it's stubborn and can be a rewarding challenge to train. The Grass-type Pokémon **Turtwig** is the same size as Piplup. The shell on Turtwig's back is made of hardened soil. If Turtwig is healthy, the shell will feel moist. If Turtwig is sick or thirsty, the leaf on its head wilts.

Fire-type **Chimchar** stands a bit taller than its peers, with a rear end that burns thanks to gas stored in its belly. If Chimchar isn't feeling well, its flame will dim. It evolves into **Monferno**, which attacks with a fiery tail! Monferno evolves into the Fire- and Fighting-type **Infernape**, one of the smallest fully evolved starter Pokémon at under 4 feet tall. Infernape's size makes it quick and

Sinnoh is home to some intriguing Pokémon, from diminutive Rotom to immense Abomasnow! One-foot-tall **Rotom** can sneak into electronic devices and cause mischief. Rotom has multiple forms that resemble several different electrical devices. The popular and well-known Fighting- and Steel-type Pokémon **Lucario** is four times taller than Rotom. Lucario can sense auras from a great distance. By reading auras, Lucario can detect feelings and even understand human speech.

Another beloved and fierce Pokémon from the Sinnoh region, **Garchomp** can fly as fast as a jet plane—and could possibly even win a race against one! Other flying Pokémon have learned that colliding with a Garchomp moving at top speed is very dangerous indeed! By contrast, the 7'03" Ice- and Grass-type Abomasnow is a gentle giant that prefers a quiet life among the snowy peaks of Sinnoh. It whips up blizzards to remain hidden and would not be described as social. . . .

Some Pokémon undergo huge size changes during evolution, growing from petite pushovers to massive monsters! Check out these unbelievable transformations.

Feebas is like a shabbier cousin to Magikarp, and is about as useless in battle. It can live in dirty or polluted water with few problems. The unattractive but remarkably hardy Feebas evolves into **Milotic**, which is said to be the most beautiful Pokémon of all. At more than 20 feet long, Milotic gives off calming energy and has inspired countless artists to produce beautiful paintings and sculptures.

Magikarp has a reputation for splashing out of the water recklessly, which leaves it helplessly open to attack. Although this Water-type Pokémon has almost no fighting skills, it flourishes throughout most regions in huge numbers. When Magikarp evolves, it becomes the terrifying **Gyarados**, which is ten times the length of Magikarp—and ten thousand times angrier! Gyarados is infamous for its temper, and will destroy everything in its path if it becomes infuriated.

WELCOME TO UNOVA!

Tepig is a Fire-type first-partner Pokémon. It doesn't care for the taste of raw berries, so it snorts flames out its nose to cook them—and often burns them to a crisp by accident! Tepig isn't the only amateur chef in Unova: the shell-like scalchop on Water-type **Oshawott**'s stomach can be used as a sharp-edged weapon during battle—or it can crack open tough food.

Grass-type Pokémon **Snivy** gathers energy from the sun by using the leaf on its tail. This calm Pokémon is better at using its vine whips than it is at using its hands. Snivy evolves into **Servine**, which evolves into **Serperior**. Serperior is the longest of all fully evolved first-partner Pokémon. It is said that a single glare from a Serperior can stop most opponents in their tracks!

Unova is home to **Litwick**, one of the smallest Ghost-type Pokémon. Litwick gains fuel through others' life force by shining its light and pretending to be a guide, but don't follow one . . . it's a trap! The Grass- and Fairy-type **Whimsicott** floats about with less ominous goals. It often breezes into homes and leaves behind balls of fluffy white cotton. But if the wind picks up again, it'll blow away!

The Dark-type Pokémon **Zoroark** stands at 5'03"—but you might never see its true form. A master of deception, Zoroark can fool large groups of people with its tricks, even appearing to opposing Trainers as entirely different Pokémon. At 9'02", the massive **Golurk** towers over most Unova natives. Luckily, it was created long ago to protect humans and other Pokémon. Take caution, though: breaking the seal on its chest would release uncontrollable energy.

WELCOME TO KALOS!

The Grass-type **Chespin** guards itself with a thick shell of nutlike wood. Its quills are usually soft and harmless, but Chespin can flex them to a dangerous point when threatened. Chespin evolves into **Quilladin**, which evolves into **Chesnaught**, the biggest fully evolved starter Pokémon from the Kalos region. Its thick shell can withstand a bomb blast! Chesnaught is known to shield its friends with its own body.

Water-type first-partner Pokémon **Froakie** may seem carefree, but this little Pokémon always keeps a watchful eye on its surroundings. The bubbles on its back help protect Froakie from harm. Fire-type **Fennekin** may not have built-in armor like Froakie and Chespin, but its large ears vent hot air that can reach searing temperatures!

Kalos is home to powerful Pokémon of all sizes. **Espurr** is only a foot tall, but its psychic energy can blast anyone within a wide radius. Espurr's ears help hide its store of psychic power and keep energy from leaking out. The Flying- and Fighting-type **Hawlucha** attacks from above so its foes can't see it coming! Thanks to its aerial advantage, 2'07" Hawlucha can go toe-to-toe with big brawlers.

According to legends in the Kalos region, **Aegislash** can sense leadership ability. It is said that Aegislash has lent its spectral powers to generations of kings and queens. After all, what's more intimidating than a 5'07" sword that can move and attack on its own! Speaking of old-time royalty: when **Tyrantrum** first roamed the world millions of years ago, its massive jaws made it nearly unstoppable. It still behaves like a king, since so few Pokémon are able to stand against its power.

WELCOME TO ALOLA!

This island region is home to three unique—and petite—first-partner Pokémon. Water-type **Popplio** blows bubbles—for fun and for combat. It works hard to control those bubbles. **Rowlet** is a Grass- and Flying-type Pokémon that attacks without making a sound. It gathers energy during the day and comes alive at night to swoop down on unsuspecting foes.

The Fire-type **Litten** does not trust easily. This fiery Pokémon collects fur by grooming itself and then shoots flaming hairballs at its foes! Litten evolves into **Torracat**, which evolves into **Incineroar**. This towering wrestler is known to completely ignore its Trainer if it's not in the mood to listen. In addition to furious kicks and punches, Incineroar attacks with scorching flames!

Poor little **Mimikyu** just wants to be popular, which is why it hides its horrifying real form under a dirty old Pikachu costume. Maybe its small size makes it shy? If you're kind enough to befriend a lonely Mimikyu, be sure not to peek at what's under its disguise—it's a tiny terror!

The Bug- and Electric-type **Vikavolt** has intimidating jaws that make up nearly half the length of its almost-5-foot-long body and allow it to focus electricity and zap its foes.

Turtonator's shell explodes on impact due to its makeup of unstable material. Between its explosive shell and the poisonous fumes and flames it can spew from its nostrils, this Pokémon can be tough to beat!

On its own, **Wishiwashi (Solo Form)** is a weak Pokémon the same size as Mimikyu. When it's threatened, though, Wishiwashi's eyes begin to moisten and shine, attracting nearby Wishiwashi to teach any bullies a surprising lesson. . . .

Behold the concentrated power of **Wishiwashi (School Form)**! By banding together, Wishiwashi can scare off even the mighty Gyarados. Some fishermen even call a school of Wishiwashi the demon of the sea.

Though it was first found in Kanto, Exeggutor prefers an island breeze—as evidenced by the Alolan Pokémon's growth to its truly exceptional size of more than 35 feet tall! As the tallest known Pokémon, **Alolan Exeggutor** has grown so much that draconic powers have awakened within it. That should cause any opponent to think twice!

At nearly 50 feet long, **Wailord** is the largest known Pokémon. It swims in pods and can dive to great depths. With its huge mouth, Wailord can swallow entire schools of smaller Pokémon whole. Wailord sightseeing is a popular activity—just be sure you're not in the splash zone when this giant leaps out of the sea!

From tiny Flabébé to towering Alolan Exeggutor, and from pocket-sized Pikachu to enormous Wailord, Pokémon around the world come in all sizes and shapes. Set out on your own journey across Kanto, Johto, Hoenn, Sinnoh, Unova, Kalos, Alola, and beyond to discover them all for yourself!